Johnny Pye and the Fool-killer
(From *Tales Before Midnight*)

By

Stephen Vincent Benét

I0673686

Copyright © 2013 Read Books Ltd.
This book is copyright and may not be
reproduced or copied in any way without
the express permission of the publisher in writing

British Library Cataloguing-in-Publication Data
A catalogue record for this book is available from the
British Library

Stephen Vincent Benét

Stephen Vincent Benét was born on 22nd July 1898 in Bethlehem, Pennsylvania, United States.

Benét was sent to the Hitchcock Military Academy at the age of ten and then continued his education at The Albany Academy in New York. He also attended Yale University where he received his M.A. in English.

Benét was an accomplished writer at an early age, having had his first book published at 17 and submitting his third volume of poetry in lieu of a thesis for his degree. During his time at Yale, he was an influential figure at the 'Yale Lit' literary magazine, and a fellow member of the Elizabethan Club. Benét was also a part-time contributor for the early Time Magazine.

Benét's involvement with the University literary scene led to a decade-long judgeship of the Yale Series of Younger Poets Competition. He is also responsible for publishing the first volumes of work by authors such as James Agee, Muriel Rukeyser, Jeremy Ingalls, and Margaret Walker. In 1931, he was elected as a fellow of the American Academy of Arts ad Sciences.

Benét's best known works are the book-length narrative poem *American Civil War, John Brown's Body* (1928), for which he won a Pulitzer Prize in 1929, and two short stories, *The Devil and Daniel Webster* (1936) and *By the Waters of Babylon* (1937). Benét won a second

Pulitzer Prize posthumously for his unfinished poem *Western Star* in 1944.

Stephen Vincent Benét died of a heart attack in New York City, on 13th March, 1943, and is buried in Evergreen Cemetery, Stonington, Conneticut.

You don't hear so much about the Fool-Killer these days, but when Johnny Pye was a boy there was a good deal of talk about him. Some said he was one kind of person, and some said another, but most people agreed that he came around fairly regular. Or, it seemed so to Johnny Pye. But then, Johnny was an adopted child, which is, maybe, why he took it so hard.

The miller and his wife had offered to raise him, after his own folks died, and that was a good deed on their part. But, as soon as he lost his baby teeth and started acting the way most boys act, they began to come down on him like thunder, which wasn't so good. They were good people, according to their lights, but their lights were terribly strict ones, and they believed that the harder you were on a youngster, the better and brighter he got. Well, that may work with some children, but it didn't with Johnny Pye.

He was sharp enough and willing enough—as sharp and willing as most boys in Martinsville. But, somehow or other, he never seemed to be able to do the right things or say the right words—at least when he was home. Treat a boy like a fool and he'll act like a fool, I say, but there's some folks need convincing. The miller and his wife thought the way to smarten Johnny was to treat him like a fool, and finally they got so he pretty much believed it himself.

And that was hard on him, for he had a boy's imagination, and maybe a little more than most. He could stand the beatings and he did. But what he couldn't stand was the way things went at the mill. I don't suppose the miller intended to do it. But, as long as Johnny Pye could remember, whenever he heard of the death of somebody he didn't like, he'd say, "Well, the Fool-Killer's come for so-and-so," and sort of smack his lips. It was, as you might say, a family joke, but the miller was a big man with a big red face, and it made a strong impression on Johnny Pye. Till, finally, he got a picture of the Fool-Killer, himself. He was a big man, too, in a checked shirt and corduroy trousers, and he went walking the ways of the world, with a hickory club that had a lump of lead in the end of it. I don't know how Johnny Pye got that picture so clear, but, to him, it was just as plain as the face of any human being in Martinsville. And, now and then, just to test it, he'd ask a grown-up person, kind of timidly, if that was the way the Fool-Killer looked. And, of course, they'd generally laugh and tell him it was. Then Johnny would wake up at night, in his room over the mill, and listen for the Fool-Killer's step on the road and wonder when he was coming. But he was brave enough not to tell anybody that.

Finally, though, things got a little more than he could bear. He'd done some boy's trick or other—let the stones grind a little fine, maybe, when the miller wanted the meal ground coarse—just carelessness, you know. But he'd gotten two whippings for it, one from the miller and one from his wife, and, at the end of it, the miller had said, "Well, Johnny Pye, the Fool-Killer ought to be along for you most any day now. For I never did see a boy that was such a fool." Johnny looked to the miller's wife to see if she believed it, too, but she just shook her head and looked serious. So he went to bed that night, but he couldn't sleep, for every time a bough rustled or the mill wheel creaked, it seemed to him it must be the Fool-Killer. And, early next morning, before anybody was up, he packed such duds as he had in a bandanna handkerchief and ran away.

He didn't really expect to get away from the Fool-Killer very long—as far as he knew, the Fool-Killer got you wherever you went. But he thought he'd give him a run for his money, at least. And when he got on the road, it was a bright spring morning, and the first peace and quiet he'd had in some time. So his spirits rose, and he chunked a stone at a bullfrog as he went along, just to show he was Johnny Pye and still doing business.

He hadn't gone more than three or four miles out of Martinsville, when he heard a buggy coming up the road behind him. He knew the Fool-Killer didn't need a buggy to catch you, so he wasn't afraid of it, but he stepped to the side of the road to let it pass. But it stopped, instead, and a black-whiskered man with a stovepipe hat looked out of it.

"Hello, bub," he said. "Is this the road for East Liberty?"

"My name's John Pye and I'm eleven years old," said Johnny, polite but firm, "and you take the next left fork for East Liberty. They say it's a pretty town—I've never been there myself." And he sighed a little, because he thought he'd like to see the world before the Fool-Killer caught up with him.

"H'm," said the man. "Stranger here, too, eh? And what brings a smart boy like you on the road so early in the morning?"

"Oh," said Johnny Pye, quite honestly, "I'm running away from the Fool-Killer. For the miller says I'm a fool and his wife says I'm a fool and almost everybody in Martinsville says I'm a fool except little Susie Marsh. And the miller says the Fool-Killer's after me—so I thought I'd run away before he came."

The black-whiskered man sat in his buggy and wheezed for a while. When he got his breath back, "Well, jump in, bub," he said. "The miller may say you're a fool, but I think you're a right smart boy to be running away from the Fool-Killer all by yourself. And I don't hold with small town prejudices and I need a right smart boy, so I'll give you a lift on the road."

"But, will I be safe from the Fool-Killer, if I'm with you?" said Johnny. "For, otherwise, it don't signify."

"Safe?" said the black-whiskered man, and wheezed again. "Oh, you'll be safe as houses. You see, I'm a herb doctor—and some folks think, a little in the Fool-Killer's line of business, myself. And I'll teach you a trade worth two of milling. So jump in, bub."

"Sounds all right the way you say it," said Johnny, "but my name's John Pye," and he jumped into the buggy. And they went rattling along toward East Liberty with the herb doctor talking and cutting jokes till Johnny thought he'd never met a pleasanter man. About half a mile from East Liberty, the doctor stopped at a spring.

"What are we stopping here for?" said Johnny Pye.

"Wait and see," said the doctor, and gave him a wink. Then he got a haircloth trunk full of empty bottles out of the back of the buggy and made Johnny fill them with spring water and label them. Then he added a pinch of pink powder to each bottle and shook them up and corked them and stowed them away.

"What's that?" said Johnny, very interested.

"That's Old Doctor Waldo's Unparalleled Universal Remedy," said the doctor, reading from the label.

"Made from the purest snake oil and secret Indian herbs, it cures rheumatism, blind staggers, headache, malaria, five kinds of fits, and spots in front of the eyes. It will also remove oil or grease stains, clean knives and silver, polish brass, and is strongly recommended as a general tonic and blood purifier. Small size, one dollar—family bottle, two dollars and a half."

"But I don't see any snake oil in it," said Johnny, puzzled, "or any secret Indian herbs."

"That's because you're not a fool," said the doctor, with another wink. "The Fool-Killer wouldn't, either. But most folks will."

And, that very same night, Johnny saw. For the doctor made his pitch in East Liberty and he did it handsome. He took a couple of flaring oil torches and stuck them on the sides of the buggy; he put on a diamond stickpin and did card tricks and told funny stories till he had the crowd goggle-eyed. As for Johnny, he let him play on the tambourine. Then he started talking about Doctor Waldo's Universal Remedy, and, with Johnny to help him, the bottles went like hot cakes. Johnny helped the doctor count the money afterward, and it was a pile.

"Well," said Johnny, "I never saw money made easier. You've got a fine trade, Doctor."

"It's cleverness does it," said the doctor, and slapped him on the back.

"Now a fool's content to stay in one place and do one thing, but the Fool-Killer never caught up with a good pitchman yet."

"Well, it's certainly lucky I met up with you," said Johnny, "and, if it's cleverness does it, I'll learn the trade or bust."

So he stayed with the doctor quite a while—in fact, till he could make up the remedy and do the card tricks almost as good as the doctor. And the doctor liked Johnny, for Johnny was a biddable boy. But one night they came into a town where things didn't go as they usually did. The crowd gathered as usual, and the doctor did his tricks. But, all the time, Johnny could see a sharp-faced little fellow going through the crowd and whispering to one man and another. Till, at last, right in the middle of the doctor's spiel, the sharp-faced fellow gave a shout of "That's him all right! I'd know them whiskers anywhere!" and, with that, the crowd growled once and began to tear slats out of the nearest fence. Well, the next thing Johnny knew, he and the doctor were being ridden out of town on a rail, with the doctor's long coattails flying at every jounce.

They didn't hurt Johnny particular—him only being a boy. But they warned 'em both never to show their faces in that town again, and then they heaved the doctor into a thistle patch and went their ways.

"Owoo!" said the doctor, "ouch!" as Johnny was helping him out of the thistle patch. "Go easy with those thistles! And why didn't you give me the office, you blame little fool?"

"Office?" said Johnny. "What office?"

"When that sharp-nosed man started snooping around," said the doctor. "I thought that infernal main street looked familiar—I was through there two years ago, selling solid gold watches for a dollar apiece."

"But the works to a solid gold watch would be worth more than that," said Johnny.

"There weren't any works," said the doctor, with a groan, "but there was a nice lively beetle inside each case and it made the prettiest tick you ever heard."

"Well, that certainly was a clever idea," said Johnny. "I'd never have thought of that."

"Clever?" said the doctor. "Ouch—it was ruination! But who'd have thought the fools would bear a grudge for two years? And now we've lost the horse and buggy, too—not to speak of the bottles and the money. Well, there's lots more tricks to be played and we'll start again."

But, though he liked the doctor, Johnny began to feel dubious. For it occurred to him that, if all the doctor's cleverness got him was being ridden out of town on a rail, he couldn't be so far away from the Fool-Killer as he thought. And, sure enough, as he was going to sleep that night, he seemed to hear the Fool-Killer's footsteps coming after him—step, step, step. He pulled his jacket up over his ears, but he couldn't shut it out. So, when the doctor had got in the way of starting business over again, he and Johnny parted company. The doctor didn't bear any grudge; he shook hands with Johnny and told him to remember that cleverness was power. And Johnny went on with his running away.

He got to a town, and there was a store with a sign in the window, BOY WANTED, so he went in. There, sure enough, was the merchant, sitting at his desk, and a fine, important man he looked, in his black broadcloth suit.

Johnny tried to tell him about the Fool-Killer, but the merchant wasn't interested in that. He just looked Johnny over and saw that he looked biddable and strong for his age. "But, remember, no fooling around, boy!" said the merchant sternly, after he'd hired him.

"No fooling around?" said Johnny, with the light of hope in his eyes.

"No," said the merchant, meaningly. "We've no room for fools in this business, I can tell you! You work hard, and you'll rise. But, if you've got any foolish notions, just knock them on the head and forget them."

Well, Johnny was glad enough to promise that, and he stayed with the merchant a year and a half. He swept out the store, and he put the shutters up and took them down; he ran errands and wrapped up packages and learned to keep busy twelve hours a day. And, being a biddable boy and an honest one, he rose, just like the merchant had said. The merchant raised his wages and let him begin to wait on customers and learn accounts. And then, one night, Johnny woke up in the middle of the night. And it seemed to him he heard, far away but getting nearer, the steps of the Fool-Killer after him—tramping, tramping.

He went to the merchant next day and said, "Sir, I'm sorry to tell you this, but I'll have to be moving on."

"Well, I'm sorry to hear that, Johnny," said the merchant, "for you've been a good boy. And, if it's a question of salary—"

"It isn't that," said Johnny, "but tell me one thing, sir, if you don't mind my asking. Supposing I did stay with you—where would I end?"

The merchant, smiled. "That's a hard question to answer," he said, "and I'm not much given to compliments. But I started, myself, as a boy, sweeping out the store. And you're a bright youngster with lots of go-ahead. I don't see why, if you stuck to it, you shouldn't make the same kind of success that I have."

"And what's that?" said Johnny.

The merchant began to look irritated, but he kept his smile.

"Well," he said, "I'm not a boastful man, but I'll tell you this. Ten years ago I was the richest man in town. Five years ago, I was the richest man in the county. And five years from now—well, I aim to be the richest man in the state."

His eyes kind of glittered as he said it, but Johnny was looking at his face. It was sallow-skinned and pouchy, with the jaw as hard as a rock. And it came upon Johnny that moment that, though he'd known the merchant a year and a half, he'd never really seen him enjoy himself except when he was driving a bargain.

"Sorry, sir," he said, "but, if it's like that, I'll certainly have to go. Because, you see, I'm running away from the Fool-Killer, and if I stayed here and got to be like you, he'd certainly catch up with me in no—"

"Why, you impertinent young cub!" roared the merchant, with his face gone red all of a sudden. "Get your money from the cashier!" and Johnny was on the road again before you could say "Jack Robinson." But, this time, he was used to it, and walked off whistling.

Well, after that, he hired out to quite a few different people, but I won't go into all of his adventures. He worked for an inventor for a while, and they split up because Johnny happened to ask him what would be the good of his patent, self-winding, perpetual-motion machine, once he did get it invented. And, while the inventor talked big about improving the human race and

15

the beauties of science, it was plain he didn't know. So that night, Johnny heard the steps of the Fool-Killer, far off but coming closer, and, next morning, he went away. Then he stayed with a minister for a while, and he certainly hated to leave him, for the minister was a good man. But they got talking one evening and, as it chanced, Johnny asked him what happened to people who didn't believe in his particular religion. Well, the minister was broad-minded, but there's only one answer to that. He admitted they might be good folks—he even admitted they mightn't exactly go to hell—but he couldn't let them into heaven, no, not the best and the wisest of them, for there were the specifications laid down by creed and church, and, if you didn't fulfill them, you didn't.

So Johnny had to leave him, and, after that, he went with an old drunken fiddler for a while. He wasn't a good man, I guess, but he could play till the tears ran down your cheeks. And, when he was playing his best, it seemed to Johnny that the Fool-Killer was very far away. For, in spite of his faults and his weaknesses, while he played, there was might in the man. But he died drunk in a ditch, one night, with Johnny to hold his head, and, while he left Johnny his fiddle, it didn't do Johnny much good. For, while Johnny could play a tune, he couldn't play like the fiddler—it wasn't in his fingers.

Then it chanced that Johnny took up with a company of soldiers. He was still too young to enlist, but they made a kind of pet of him, and everything went swimmingly for a while. For the captain was the bravest man Johnny had ever seen, and he had an answer for everything, out of regulations and the Articles of War. But then they went West to fight Indians and the same old trouble cropped up again. For one night the captain said to him, "Johnny, we're going to fight the enemy tomorrow, but you'll stay in camp."

"Oh, I don't want to do that," said Johnny; "I want to be in on the fighting."

"It's an order," said the captain, grimly. Then he gave Johnny certain instructions and a letter to take to his wife.

"For the colonel's a copper-plated fool," he said, "and we're walking straight into an ambush."

"Why don't you tell him that?" said Johnny.

"I have," said the captain, "but he's the colonel."

"Colonel or no colonel," said Johnny, "if he's a fool, somebody ought to stop him."

"You can't do that, in an army," said the captain. "Orders are orders." But it turned out the captain was wrong about it, for, next day, before they could get moving, the Indians attacked and got badly licked. When it was all over, "Well, it was a good fight," said the captain, professionally. "All the same, if they'd waited

17

and laid an ambush, they'd have had our hair. But, as it was, they didn't stand a chance."

"But why didn't they lay an ambush?" said Johnny.

"Well," said the captain, "I guess they had their orders too. And now, how would you like to be a soldier?"

"Well, it's a nice outdoors life, but I'd like to think it over," said Johnny. For he knew the captain was brave and he knew the Indians had been brave—you couldn't find two braver sets of people. But, all the same, when he thought the whole thing over, he seemed to hear steps in the sky. So he soldiered to the end of the campaign and then he left the army, though the captain told him he was making a mistake.

By now, of course, he wasn't a boy any longer; he was getting to be a young man with a young man's thoughts and feelings. And, half the time, nowadays, he'd forget about the Fool-Killer except as a dream he'd had when he was a boy. He could even laugh at it now and then, and think what a fool he'd been to believe there was such a man.

But, all the same, the desire in him wasn't satisfied, and something kept driving him on. He'd have called it ambitiousness, now, but it came to the same thing. And with every new trade he tried, sooner or later would come the dream—the dream of the big man in the checked shirt and corduroy pants, walking the ways of the world with his hickory stick in one hand. It made him angry to have that dream, now, but it had a singular power over him. Till, finally, when he was turned twenty or so, he got scared.

"Fool-Killer or no Fool-Killer," he said to himself. "I've got to ravel this matter out. For there must be some one thing a man could tie to, and be sure he wasn't a fool. I've tried cleverness and money and half a dozen other things, and they don't seem to be the answer. So now I'll try book learning and see what comes of that."

So he read all the books he could find, and whenever he'd seem to hear the steps of the Fool-Killer coming for the authors—and that was frequent—he'd try and shut his ears. But some books said one thing was best and some another, and he couldn't rightly decide.

"Well," he said to himself, when he'd read and read till his head felt as stuffed with book learning as a sausage with meat, "it's interesting, but it isn't exactly contemporaneous. So I think I'll go down to Washington and ask the wise men there. For it must take a lot of wisdom to run a country like the United States, and if there's people who can answer my questions, it's there they ought to be found."

So he packed his bag and off to Washington he went. He was modest for a youngster, and he didn't intend to try and see the President right away. He thought probably a congressman was about his size. So he saw a congressman, and the congressman told him the thing to be was an upstanding young American and vote the Republican ticket—which sounded all right to Johnny Pye, but not exactly what he was after.

Then he went to a senator, and the senator told him to be an upstanding young American and vote the Democratic ticket—which sounded all right, too, but not what he was after, either. And, somehow, though both men had been impressive and affable, right in the middle of their speeches he'd seemed to hear steps—you know.

But a man has to eat, whatever else he does, and Johnny found he'd better buckle down and get himself a job. It happened to be with the first congressman he struck, for that one came from Martinsville, which is why Johnny went to him in the first place. And, in a little while, he forgot his search entirely and the Fool-Killer, too, for the congressman's niece came East to visit him, and she was the Susie Marsh that Johnny had sat next in school. She'd been pretty then, but she was prettier now, and as soon as Johnny Pye saw her, his heart gave a jump and a thump.

"And don't think we don't remember you in Martinsville, Johnny Pye," she said, when her uncle had explained who his new clerk was. "Why, the whole town'll be excited when I write home. We've heard all about your killing Indians and inventing perpetual motion and traveling around the country with a famous doctor and making a fortune in dry goods and—oh, it's a wonderful story!"

"Well," said Johnny, and coughed, "some of that's just a little bit exaggerated. But it's nice of you to be interested. So they don't think I'm a fool any more, in Martinsville?"

"I never thought you were a fool," said Susie with a little smile, and Johnny felt his heart give another bump.

"And I always knew you were pretty, but never how pretty till now," said Johnny, and coughed again. "But, speaking of old times, how's the miller and his wife? For I did leave them right sudden, and while there were faults on both sides, I must have been a trial to them too."

"They've gone the way of all flesh," said Susie Marsh, "and there's a new miller now. But he isn't very well-liked, to tell the truth, and he's letting the mill run down."

"That's a pity," said Johnny, "for it was a likely mill." Then he began to ask her more questions and she began to remember things too. Well, you know how the time can go when two youngsters get talking like that.

Johnny Pye never worked so hard in his life as he did that winter. And it wasn't the Fool-Killer he thought about—it was Susie Marsh. First he thought she loved him and then he was sure she didn't, and then he was betwixt and between, and all perplexed and confused. But, finally, it turned out all right and he had her promise, and Johnny Pye knew he was the happiest man in the world. And that night, he waked up in the night and heard the Fool-Killer coming after him—step, step, step.

He didn't sleep much after that, and he came down to breakfast hollow-eyed. But his uncle-to-be didn't notice that—he was rubbing his hands and smiling.

"Put on your best necktie, Johnny!" he said, very cheerful, "for I've got an appointment with the President today, and, just to show I approve of my niece's fiancé, I'm taking you along."

"The President!" said Johnny, all dumfounded.

"Yes," said Congressman Marsh, "you see, there's a little bill—well, we needn't go into that. But slick down your back hair, Johnny—we'll make Martinsville proud of us this day!"

Then a weight seemed to go from Johnny's shoulders and a load from his heart. He wrung Mr. Marsh's hand.

"Thank you, Uncle Eben!" he said. "I can't thank you enough." For, at last, he knew he was going to look upon a man that was bound to be safe from the Fool-Killer—and it seemed to him if he could just once do that, all his troubles and searchings would be ended.

Well, it doesn't signify which President it was—you can take it from me that he was President and a fine-looking man. He'd just been elected, too, so he was lively as a trout, and the saddle galls he'd get from Congress hadn't even begun to show. Anyhow, there he was, and Johnny feasted his eyes on him. For if there was anybody in the country the Fool-Killer couldn't bother, it must be a man like this.

The President and the congressman talked politics for a while, and then it was Johnny's turn.

"Well, young man," said the President, affably, "and what can I do for you—for you look to me like a fine, upstanding young American."

The congressman cut in quick before Johnny could open his mouth.

"Just a word of advice, Mr. President," he said. "Just a word in season. For my young friend's led an adventurous life, but now he's going to marry my niece and settle down. And what he needs most of all is a word of ripe wisdom from you."

"Well," said the President, looking at Johnny rather keenly, "if that's all he needs, a short horse is soon curried. I wish most of my callers wanted as little."

But, all the same, he drew Johnny out, as such men can, and before Johnny knew it, he was telling his life story.

"Well," said the President, at the end, "you certainly have been a rolling stone, young man. But there's nothing wrong in that. And, for one of your varied experience there's one obvious career. Politics!" he said, and slapped his fist in his hand.

"Well," said Johnny, scratching his head, "of course, since I've been in Washington, I've thought of that. But I don't know that I'm rightly fitted."

"You can write a speech," said Congressman Marsh, quite thoughtful, "for you've helped me with mine. You're a likeable fellow too. And you were born poor and worked up—and you've even got a war record—why, hell! Excuse me, Mr. President!—he's worth five hundred votes just as he stands!"

"I—I'm more than honored by you two gentlemen," said Johnny, abashed and flattered, "but supposing I did go into politics—where would I end up?"

The President looked sort of modest.

"The Presidency of the United States," said he, "is within the legitimate ambition of every American citizen. Provided he can get elected, of course."

"Oh," said Johnny, feeling dazzled, "I never thought of that. Well, that's a great thing. But it must be a great responsibility too."

"It is," said the President, looking just like his pictures on the campaign buttons.

"Why, it must be an awful responsibility!" said Johnny. "I can't hardly see how a mortal man can bear it. Tell me, Mr. President," he said, "may I ask you a question?"

"Certainly," said the President, looking prouder and more responsible and more and more like his picture on the campaign buttons every minute.

"Well," said Johnny, "it sounds like a fool question, but it's this: This is a great big country of ours, Mr. President, and it's got the most amazing lot of different people in it. How can any President satisfy all those people at one time? Can you yourself, Mr. President?"

The President looked a bit taken aback for a minute. But then he gave Johnny Pye a statesman's glance.

"With the help of God," he said, solemnly, "and in accordance with the principles of our great party, I intend . . ."

But Johnny didn't even hear the end of the sentence. For, even as the President was speaking, he heard a step outside in the corridor and he knew, somehow, it wasn't the step of a secretary or a guard. He was glad the President had said "with the help of God" for that sort of softened the step. And when the President finished, Johnny bowed.

"Thank you, Mr. President," he said; "that's what I wanted to know. And now I'll go back to Martinsville, I guess."

"Go back to Martinsville?" said the President, surprised.

"Yes, sir," said Johnny. "For I don't think I'm cut out for politics."

"And is that all you have to say to the President of the United States?" said his uncle-to-be, in a fume.

But the President had been thinking, meanwhile, and he was a bigger man than the congressman.

"Wait a minute, Congressman," he said. "This young man's honest, at least, and I like his looks. Moreover, of all the people who've come to see me in the last six months, he's the only one who hasn't wanted something—except the White House cat, and I guess she wanted something, too, because she meowed. You don't want to be President, young man—and, confidentially, I don't blame you. But how would you like to be postmaster at Martinsville?"

"Postmaster at Martinsville?" said Johnny. "But—"

"Oh, it's only a tenth-class post office," said the President, "but, for once in my life, I'll do something because I want to, and let Congress yell its head off. Come—is it yes or no?"

Johnny thought of all the places he'd been and all the trades he'd worked at. He thought, queerly enough, of the old drunk fiddler dead in the ditch, but he knew he couldn't be that. Mostly, though, he thought of Martinsville and Susie Marsh. And, though he'd just heard the Fool-Killer's step, he defied the Fool-Killer.

"Why, it's yes, of course, Mr. President," he said, "for then I can marry Susie."

"That's as good a reason as you'll find," said the President. "And now, I'll just write a note."

Well, he was as good as his word, and Johnny and his Susie were married and went back to live in Martinsville. And, as soon as Johnny learned the ways of postmastering, he found it as good a trade as most. There wasn't much mail in Martinsville, but, in between whiles, he ran the mill, and that was a good trade too. And all the time, he knew, at the back of his mind, that he hadn't quite settled accounts with the Fool-Killer. But he didn't much care about that, for he and Susie were happy. And after a while they had a child, and that was the most remarkable experience that had ever happened to any young couple, though the doctor said it was a perfectly normal baby.

One evening, when his son was about a year old. Johnny Pye took the river road, going home. It was a mite longer than the hill road, but it was the cool of the evening, and there's times when a man likes to walk by himself, fond as he may be of his wife and family.

He was thinking of the way things had turned out for him, and they seemed to him pretty astonishing and singular, as they do to most folks, when you think them over. In fact, he was thinking so hard that, before he knew it, he'd almost stumbled over an old scissors grinder who'd set up his grindstone and tools by the side of the road. The scissors grinder had his cart with him, but he'd turned the horse out to graze—and a lank, old, white horse it was, with every rib showing. And he was very busy, putting an edge on a scythe.

"Oh, sorry," said Johnny Pye. "I didn't know anybody was camping here. But you might come around to my house tomorrow—my wife's got some knives that need sharpening."

Then he stopped, for the old man gave him a long, keen look.

"Why, it's you, Johnny Pye," said the old man. "And how do you do, Johnny Pye! You've been a long time coming—in fact, now and then, I thought I'd have to fetch you. But you're here at last."

Johnny Pye was a grown man now, but he began to tremble.

"But it isn't you!" he said, wildly. "I mean you're not him! Why, I've known how he looks all my life! He's a big man, with a checked shirt, and he carries a hickory stick with a lump of lead in one end."

"Oh, no," said the scissors grinder, quite quiet. "You may have thought of me that way, but that's not the way I am." And Johnny Pye heard the scythe go whet-whet-whet on the stone. The old man ran some water on it and looked at the edge. Then he shook his head as if the edge didn't quite satisfy him. "Well, Johnny, are you ready?" he said, after a while.

"Ready?" said Johnny, in a hoarse voice. "Of course I'm not ready."

"That's what they all say," said the old man, nodding his head, and the scythe went whet-whet on the stone.

Johnny wiped his brow and started to argue it out.

"You see, if you'd found me earlier," he said, "or later. I don't want to be unreasonable, but I've got a wife and a child."

"Most has wives and many has children," said the old man, grimly, and the scythe went whet-whet on the stone as he pushed the treadle. And a shower of sparks flew, very clear and bright, for the night had begun to fall.

"Oh, stop that damn racket and let a man think for a minute!" said Johnny, desperate. "I can't go, I tell you. I won't. It isn't time. It's—"

The old man stopped the grindstone and pointed with the scythe at Johnny Pye.

"Tell me one good reason," he said. "There's men would be missed in the world, but are you one of them? A clever man might be missed, but are you a clever man?"

"No," said Johnny, thinking of the herb doctor. "I had a chance to be clever, but I gave it up."

"One," said the old man, ticking off on his fingers. "Well, a rich man might be missed—by some. But you aren't rich, I take it."

"No," said Johnny, thinking of the merchant, "nor wanted to be."

"Two," said the old man. "Cleverness—riches—they're done. But there's still martial bravery and being a hero. There might be an argument to make, if you were one of those."

Johnny Pye shuddered a little, remembering the way that battlefield had looked, out West, when the Indians were dead and the fight over.

"No," he said, "I've fought, but I'm not a hero."

"Well, then, there's religion," said the old man, sort of patient, "and science, and—but what's the use? We know what you did with those. I might feel a trifle of compunction if I had to deal with a President of the United States. But—"

"Oh, you know well enough I ain't President," said Johnny, with a groan. "Can't you get it over with and be done?"

"You're not putting up a very good case," said the old man, shaking his head. "I'm surprised at you, Johnny. Here you spend your youth running away from being a fool. And yet, what's the first thing you do, when you're man grown? Why, you marry a girl, settle down in your home town, and start raising children when you don't know how they'll turn out. You might have known I'd catch up with you, then—you just put yourself in my way."

"Fool I may be," said Johnny Pye in his agony, "and if you take it like that, I guess we're all fools. But Susie's my wife, and my child's my child. And, as for work in the world—well, somebody has to be postmaster, or folks wouldn't get the mail."

"Would it matter much if they didn't?" said the old man, pointing his scythe.

"Well, no, I don't suppose it would, considering what's on the post cards," said Johnny Pye. "But while it's my business to sort it, I'll sort it as well as I can."

The old man whetted his scythe so hard that a long shower of sparks flew out on the grass.

"Well," he said, "I've got my job, too, and I do it likewise. But I'll tell you what I'll do. You're coming my way, no doubt of it, but, looking you over, you don't look quite ripe yet. So I'll let you off for a while. For that matter," said he, "if you'll answer one question of mine—how a man can be a human being and not be a fool—I'll let you off permanent. It'll be the first time in history," he said, "but you've got to do something on your own hook, once in a while. And now you can walk along, Johnny Pye."

With that he grounded the scythe till the sparks flew out like the tail of a comet and Johnny Pye walked along. The air of the meadow had never seemed so sweet to him before.

All the same, even with his relief, he didn't quite forget, and sometimes Susie had to tell the children not to disturb father because he was thinking. But time went ahead, as it does, and pretty soon Johnny Pye found he was forty. He'd never expected to be forty, when he was young, and it kind of surprised him. But there it was, though he couldn't say he felt much different, except now and then when he stooped over. And he was a solid citizen of the town, well-liked and well-respected, with a growing family and a stake in the community, and when he thought those things over, they kind of surprised him too. But, pretty soon, it was as if things had always been that way.

It was after his eldest son had been drowned out fishing that Johnny Pye met the scissors grinder again. But this time he was bitter and distracted, and, if he could have got to the old man, he'd have done him a mortal harm. But, somehow or other, when he tried to come to grips with him, it was like reaching for air and mist. He could see the sparks fly from the ground scythe, but he couldn't even touch the wheel.

"You coward!" said Johnny Pye. "Stand up and fight like a man!" But the old man just nodded his head and the wheel kept grinding and grinding.

"Why couldn't you have taken me?" said Johnny Pye, as if those words had never been said before. "What's the sense in all this? Why can't you take me now?"

Then he tried to wrench the scythe from the old man's hands, but he couldn't touch it. And then he fell down and lay on the grass for a while.

"Time passes," said the old man, nodding his head. "Time passes."

"It will never cure the grief I have for my son," said Johnny Pye.

"It will not," said the old man, nodding his head. "But time passes. Would you leave your wife a widow and your other children fatherless for the sake of your grief?"

"No, God help me!" said Johnny Pye. "That wouldn't be right for a man."

"Then go home to your house, Johnny Pye," said the old man. And Johnny Pye went, but there were lines in his face that hadn't been there before.

And time passed, like the flow of the river, and Johnny Pye's children married and had houses and children of their own. And Susie's hair grew white, and her back grew bent, and when Johnny Pye and his children followed her to her grave, folks said she'd died in the fullness of years, but that was hard for Johnny Pye to believe. Only folks didn't talk as plain as they used to, and the sun didn't heat as much, and sometimes, before dinner, he'd go to sleep in his chair.

And once, after Susie had died, the President of those days came through Martinsville and Johnny Pye shook hands with him and there was a piece in the paper about his shaking hands with two Presidents, fifty years apart. Johnny Pye cut out the clipping and kept it in his pocketbook. He liked this President all right, but, as he told people, he wasn't a patch on the other one fifty years ago. Well, you couldn't expect it—you didn't have Presidents these days, not to call them Presidents. All the same, he took a lot of satisfaction in the clipping.

He didn't get down to the river road much any more—it wasn't too long a walk, of course, but he just didn't often feel like it. But, one day, he slipped away from the granddaughter that was taking care of him, and went. It was kind of a steep road, really—he didn't remember its being so steep.

"Well," said the scissors grinder, "and good afternoon to you, Johnny Pye."

"You'll have to talk a little louder," said Johnny Pye. "My hearing's perfect, but folks don't speak as plain as they used to. Stranger in town?"

"Oh, so that's the way it is," said the scissors grinder.

"Yes, that's the way it is," said Johnny Pye. He knew he ought to be afraid of this fellow, now he'd put on his spectacles and got a good look at him, but for the life of him, he couldn't remember why.

"I know just who you are," he said, a little fretfully. "Never forgot a face in my life, and your name's right on the tip of my tongue—"

"Oh, don't bother about names," said the scissors grinder. "We're old acquaintances. And I asked you a question, years ago—do you remember that?"

"Yes," said Johnny Pye, "I remember." Then he began to laugh—a high, old man's laugh. "And of all the fool questions I ever was asked," he said, "that certainly took the cake."

"Oh?" said the scissors grinder.

"Uh-huh," said Johnny Pye. "For you asked me how a man could be a human being and yet not be a fool. And the answer is—when he's dead and gone and buried. Any fool would know that."

"That so?" said the scissors grinder.

"Of course," said Johnny Pye. "I ought to know. I'll be ninety-two next November, and I've shook hands with two Presidents. The first President I shook—"

"I'll be interested to hear about that," said the scissors grinder, "but we've got a little business, first. For, if all human beings are fools, how does the world get ahead?"

"Oh, there's lots of other things," said Johnny Pye, kind of impatient. "There's the brave and the wise and the clever—and they're apt to roll it ahead as much as an inch. But it's all mixed in together. For, Lord, it's only some fool kind of creature that would have crawled out of the sea to dry land in the first place—or got dropped from the Garden of Eden, if you like it better that way. You can't depend on the kind of folks people think they are—you've got to go by what they do. And I wouldn't give much for a man that some folks hadn't thought was a fool, in his time."

"Well," said the scissors grinder, "you've answered my question—at least as well as you could, which is all you can expect of a man. So I'll keep my part of the bargain."

"And what was that?" said Johnny. "For, while it's all straight in my head, I don't quite recollect the details."

"Why," said the scissors grinder, rather testy, "I'm to let you go, you old fool! You'll never see me again till the Last Judgment. There'll be trouble in the office about it," said he, "but you've got to do what you like, once in a while."

"Phew!" said Johnny Pye. "That needs thinking over!" And he scratched his head.

"Why?" said the scissors grinder, a bit affronted. "It ain't often I offer a man eternal life."

"Well," said Johnny Pye, "I take it very kind, but, you see, it's this way." He thought for a moment. "No," he said, "you wouldn't understand. You can't have touched seventy yet, by your looks, and no young man would."

"Try me," said the scissors grinder.

"Well," said Johnny Pye, "it's this way," and he scratched his head again. "I'm not saying—if you'd made the offer forty years ago, or even twenty. But, well, now, let's just take one detail. Let's say 'teeth.'"

"Well, of course," said the scissors grinder, "naturally—I mean you could hardly expect me to do anything about that."

"I thought so," said Johnny Pye. "Well, you see, these are good, bought teeth, but I'm sort of tired of hearing them click. And spectacles, I suppose, the same?"

"I'm afraid so," said the scissors grinder. "I can't interfere with time, you know—that's not my department. And, frankly, you couldn't expect, at a hundred and eighty, let's say, to be quite the man you was at ninety. But still, you'd be a wonder!"

"Maybe so," said Johnny Pye, "but, you see—well, the truth is, I'm an old man now. You wouldn't think it to look at me, but it's so. And my friends—well, they're gone—and Susie and the boy—and somehow you don't get as close to the younger people, except the children. And to keep on just going and going till Judgment Day, with nobody around to talk to that had real horse sense—well, no, sir, it's a handsome offer but I just don't feel up to accepting it. It may not be patriotic of me, and I feel sorry for Martinsville. It'd do wonders for the climate and the chamber of commerce to have a leading citizen live till Judgment Day. But a man's got to do as he likes, at least once in his life." He stopped and looked at the scissors grinder. "I'll admit, I'd kind of like to beat out Ike Leavis," he said. "To hear him talk, you'd think nobody had ever pushed ninety before. But I suppose—"

"I'm afraid we can't issue a limited policy," said the scissors grinder.

"Well," said Johnny Pye, "I just thought of it. And Ike's all right." He waited a moment. "Tell me," he said, in a low voice. "Well, you know what I mean. Afterwards. I mean, if you're likely to see"—he coughed—"your friends again. I mean, if it's so—like some folks believe."

"I can't tell you that," said the scissors grinder. "I only go so far."

"Well, there's no harm in asking," said Johnny Pye, rather humbly. He peered into the darkness; a last shower of sparks flew from the scythe, then the whir of the wheel stopped.

"H'm," said Johnny Pye, testing the edge. "That's a well-ground scythe. But they used to grind 'em better in the old days." He listened and looked, for a moment, anxiously. "Oh, Lordy!" he said, "there's Helen coming to look for me. She'll take me back to the house."

"Not this time," said the scissors grinder. "Yes, there isn't bad steel in that scythe. Well, let's go, Johnny Pye."

THE END

www.ingramcontent.com/pod-product-compliance
Lightning Source LLC
Chambersburg PA
CBHW020706260626
47157CB00008B/3166